IF I Were A King
IF I Were A Queen

Cover portrait: A king and queen from the Ivory Coast

Milet Publishing Ltd
6 North End Parade
London W14 OSJ
England
Email info@milet.com
Website www.milet.com

First published by
Milet Publishing Ltd in 2002

© Véronique Tadjo 2002
© Milet Publishing Ltd 2002

ISBN 1 84059 339 3

Printed in Belgium

Other Milet titles by Véronique Tadjo
Mamy Wata and the Monster
The Lucky Grain of Corn
Grandma Nana

Véronique Tadjo

IF I Were A King
IF I Were A Queen

Milet

A king from Dahomey

If I were a king,
I would have a huge palace
and a big treasure.
Many people would try their best
to please me.

A queen from Ghana

If I were a queen,
I would sit all day long
doing nothing
and drinking fresh coconut juice
in the shade.

A king from Morocco

If I were a king,
I would not have
to go to school anymore.
I would just wave my sword
and order everybody around.

A queen from Gabon

If I were a queen,
I would be as tall as my mother.
Nobody would dare tell me off!
I would have anything I wanted.

A Zulu king
from South Africa

If I were a king,
at night, I would fall asleep easily.
I would not be afraid
of all the shadows living in the dark.
I would be the bravest of all!

A queen from Egypt

If I were a queen,
I would tell the birds
to make mornings come sooner.
Their whistling
would encourage the sun
to rise, rise, rise,
high in the sky.

A king from Congo

If I were a king,
I would fight to protect nature
and I would respect
the animal kingdom.

A princess from Rwanda

If I were a queen,
I would paint cities
with bright colours.
I would let flowers grow
and create lots of parks
so people could dream and
play in the grass.

A sultan from Nigeria

If I were a king,
I would abolish poverty.
There would be no street children,
no more beggars.

A queen from Benin

If I were a queen,
I would immediately
stop all wars.

A king from Uganda

If I were a king,
I would ask children
to be friends with one another
and I would ask grown-ups
to do their best to stay united.

A queen from Madagascar

If I were a queen,
there would be
no North nor South,
no East nor West.
There would just be
one nation, one world.